103635

745.5
BJO

Bjork, Christina.

Linnea's almanac

LINNEA'S ALMANAC

Text Christina Björk
Drawings Lena Anderson

For Nicolina, Kalle, Pelle and Olof

R&S BOOKS

Stockholm   New York   London   Adelaide

Hi! My name is Linnea

I am named after the linnaea, a little pink woodland flower. I'm no woodland flower, though – I'm an asphalt flower. I live right in the middle of the city, but I love plants and flowers and everything that grows. So a city isn't such a great place for someone like me, right? Wrong. All over my room, things are growing.

My friend Mr. Bloom taught me all about plants. He's a retired gardener who lives in my building. Mr. Bloom has a green thumb. It's not actually green. That just means he's good at making things grow.

Mr. Brush also has a green thumb. (Sometimes it's even blue, because his job is to mix paints at the paint store in our building.) Mr. Bloom and Mr. Brush have known each other a long time.

They played together on this street when they were kids.

Mr. Brush has a little house with a garden that he rents just outside the city. He can grow whatever he wants there. I usually go along and help him.

I have another friend, too. It's a tree friend, the maple that grows outside my bedroom window.

For Christmas I got a book called *The Old Farmer's Almanac.* I use it almost every day. It tells you what time the sun will rise and set, when you can see the moon and the planets, and when to expect a comet. There is a weather forecast for the whole year, with dates for the first and last frost. You can write down what the weather is really like, and see if the book is correct.

And now I'll tell you about my year, month by month, what I did and what I observed. (There will be a city bird for every month, too.) Seasons are not the same everywhere. The farther south you are, the earlier spring comes, for example. But this is what it's like where *I* live.

Mr. Bloom

Mr. Brush

When it's cold and snowing outside, I always wonder how the birds will find anything to eat. This year I decided to help out by opening a bird restaurant. There are different things on the menu. But once I start, I've got to keep it up all winter, because the birds get used to it and forget how to find food by themselves. I wonder who will come to my restaurant . . .

The art of feeding winter birds

Remember: Never *stop* feeding the birds until winter is over. But don't *start* too early either, because then you might fool some migratory birds into staying, and they can't stand the cold. I usually start around Christmastime (a little earlier if it's really cold).

In the city, you can't put out food for the birds on the ground (then the rats come), so I feed them from my window.

Birdhouses aren't as good as bird feeders, where the birds can sit around the edge without getting their droppings into the food. Bird droppings can spread diseases, such as salmonellosis (food poisoning), that birds most often die of.

Seeds for a feeder are sold at plant nurseries, pet stores, or supermarkets.

Feeders have to be refilled every now and then.

Who eats what?

	fresh bread	hempseed	sunflower seeds	oats	wild birdseed	raisins	apple cores	boiled potatoes	cocoa butter	suet (tallow)	mild cheese	nuts
finch		X	X		X							
cardinal			X		X							
sparrow	X	X										X
blackbird						X	X	X				
titmouse		X	X						X	X	X	X

Pigeons, crows, magpies, and gulls eat everything they're offered.

Other bird goodies:
Unshelled peanuts,
apple cores,
coconut halves (split them with a hammer and chisel),
or nuts (in a plastic net) on a string.

Dangerous for birds:
moldy, spicy or salty foods!

My titmouse bell

I looked for a strong stick that would fit snugly into the hole of a well-washed flowerpot (not too large). There must be no cracks around the hole in the bottom. I melted a package of cocoa butter in a pan. Suet, the white fat from meat, works as well. I added some birdseed to the melted fat and let it swell up, but not harden.

Then I poured a little in the bottom of the flowerpot. When it was hard, I poured in a little more and let that harden, too. Nothing should leak out the hole. It works best if you take your time. Finally I poured in everything that was left and put it in the refrigerator, stick and all. When all the fat was hard, the titmouse bell was ready to hang up.

It took a while for the birds to discover it, but then lots of titmice came, especially the great tit, who loves fat in the winter.

The house sparrow

House sparrows are a common sight at my bird restaurant and throughout most of the world. They are true year-round city birds. They used to be even more common when they lived on the seeds found in horse manure. But now there are no horses in the city. House sparrows build their nests under roof tiles and in air vents. They have between ten and fifteen young every year, but only the ones which learn to watch out for city dangers survive. House sparrows live in flocks, all doing the same thing at the same time. I've noticed that they either all stay where they are or all fly away.

House sparrows who live in the city are much dirtier than their relatives in the country.

The female house sparrow is lighter in color than the male.

9

This is how city birds live

If you think how warm a down jacket is, then you'll understand how warmly "dressed" birds are with all their down and feathers. But the smaller a bird is, the more it has to eat to survive the winter. A little bird has to eat twice its weight every day. That much "fuel" is needed to keep its tiny body warm.

In the winter, food is hard to find. There are no insects (they're sleeping), no seeds (they're buried under the snow), and no water (it's turned to ice).

That's why many birds fly to warmer places for the winter. But some stay, in spite of everything. They've learned survival tricks, such as moving into the city and getting on "bird welfare" in the parks and by the water, where they are fed.

I usually go to one place where the water never freezes. Seven sacks of food are put out for the birds there every day during the colder months. But the sacks are not filled just with bread crumbs — that would make the birds sick. Bird-seed, suet, and lime are added, so the birds will get their vitamins.

I usually bring my own bag with *fresh bread, boiled potatoes, chopped white cabbage or lettuce, and birdseed.*

Some birds are marked with a numbered band on one leg. That way you can see if the same bird returns year after year. One swan came back every year for twenty years! But that was a record for swans.

Feed water birds in the water!
Don't try to get them to come up on land, where they can be run over.

FEBRUARY

This is the month to stay indoors and repot your plants. They aren't growing just now, and when they are resting they can stand being repotted. I usually water them a few hours ahead of time and then knock the soil ball out of the pot. If the roots are pressing against the sides of the pot, it is high time for a larger one. Outside, it's cold and not much is happening. At least, that's what I thought . . .

What's happening under the snow?

I went with Mr. Brush out to his garden. As soon as we got there, his two titmice came flying. They are almost tame and they know that Mr. Brush always has seeds in his pocket. They eat right out of his hand, but not out of mine. Not yet.

Except for the titmice, there wasn't much happening.

"Seems pretty dead around here," I said.

"Not at all," said Mr. Brush. "Lots of things are going on."

"*Where?*" I asked.

"Under the snow," he said. "That's

The great titmouse

Great titmice like suet. They are the largest and most common of the titmice and are found not only in Mr. Brush's garden but also on my windowsill. Titmice are good at climbing on my titmouse bell and the other goodies that I hang out for them.

I think titmice are a little smarter than other small birds. It's usually a tit-

mouse who chirps a warning if there's any danger. But sometimes it fools the other birds by getting them to fly away in fright, leaving the titmouse alone with the food.

The titmouse is already singing his *"sissi-ty, sissi-ty,"* so it feels as if spring can't be far away.

why I never cut the grass in the fall. Then when the snow covers the grass, there will be nice little warm places between the snow and the ground.

"And there all kinds of things are going on," Mr. Brush explained. "Mice and voles scoot back and forth in the tunnels they've chewed and dug in the grass. They have nests under there and winter storehouses full of nuts and seeds and other things. Down in the soil, under the mice and voles, are all the insects, worms, fungi, and bacteria at work turning the fallen leaves and dead plants into rich new soil."

"But what are the ants doing?"

"The ants stay way down in their deepest tunnels, where the frost can't reach them. They huddle together and keep each other warm."

"Watch out!" Mr. Brush shouted. "Don't step on that pile of leaves. The porcupine is sleeping in there."

"Well, you may wake him up with your shouting, then."

"No," said Mr. Brush, "he won't wake up. He's not *just* sleeping; he's hibernating until next spring."

"Doesn't he even come out to eat?"

"No, he lives on what he ate last fall. But he has to conserve energy: his heartbeat is slow; his breathing is weak; and his body temperature is just a few degrees above freezing."

"Look, the mice have moved in," said Mr. Brush when we went into the house.

He was right. There, on the floor, were some small mouse droppings. Mr. Brush put some hazelnuts out on the floor for the mice.

"Next time we're here, you'll see how they've opened the nuts," said Mr. Brush. "They chew holes in the pointed ends. That is, unless they turn out to be voles. Then they chew holes in the rounded ends."

"What if they take the nuts with them down into their tunnels?" I asked.

"Well, then we'll never know if we have mice or voles," said Mr. Brush.

MICE CHEW LIKE THIS ...
... VOLES, LIKE THIS

13

Time to repot

I soaked a new clay pot in water for a couple of hours so it wouldn't suck up all the plant's water. I had already bought a bag of potting soil at a nursery.

I started with my Busy Lizzie. Oh no! There was hardly any soil left in the old pot, just a lot of roots. It was the last chance for repotting.

First I covered the hole in the bottom of the new pot with a pot shard. Then I poured in a little soil and put in my Busy

Lizzie, root ball and all. She was at just the right height in her new pot. I added some more soil around her root ball and on the top. I usually use a tablespoon. Press the soil down, but not too hard (air has to be able to get to the roots). There was room for a little more soil, but I stopped about an inch from the top, to leave room for water. After a couple of hours, I threw away the extra water that had drained out into the saucer underneath the pot.

Lizzie's old pot was just the right size for my avocado plant. But first I scrubbed the pot well with detergent and a brush, rinsing it afterwards.

Bugs, ugh!

Plants think the air indoors is much too dry at this time of year. But not bugs – they love it! And it's right about now that they start showing up. I usually check under the leaves to see if I can spot any, and I give all my plants a warm tub shower once a week. Sometimes I spray them with water from a spray bottle. I hope I don't get bugs this year . . .

A magnifying glass is good to have

for spotting lice. And for examining snowflakes. They look like tiny crystal stars, each with a different pattern. I think I'll draw some of them.

14

MARCH

There's something special about branches. The city's trees are being pruned right now, so they'll grow stronger and thicker. I brought some of the branches inside and put them in a jar of cold water, which I changed every other day. It wasn't long before the branches had small pale green leaves on them. It was spring indoors! But when will spring really come???

15

Hooray! The first spring flower

Mr. Bloom and I went out looking for spring. We saw no signs of it, even though the snow had melted. Everything just looked messy – snarls of last year's grass, muddy paths, bare branches. We walked through the park to the little bridge over the brook. All the melted snow had turned the brook into a river.

I stood on the bridge and tossed in a stick. It floated away, going under the bridge and then coming right out again on the other side.

"Let's see whose stick comes out first," I said.

Mr. Bloom and I spent a long time throwing sticks in the water. Sometimes mine won; sometimes his.

And then suddenly I saw spring! I spotted something yellow by the water's edge: the first spring flower! That's for Mr. Bloom!

"How nice! Thank you, Linnea," said Mr. Bloom. "Do you know what it's called?"

"Of course," I said. "It's a coltsfoot."

"That's right," said Mr. Bloom. "And its Latin family name is *Tussilago.*"

"What's its first name?"

"*Farfara,*" said Mr. Bloom. "But you always say the last name first."

"Then it's *Tussilago farfara,*" I said. "That's a funny name."

"It's very practical to have Latin names," said Mr. Bloom, "because they're used all over the world. Animals

The game is called "Poohsticks." Pooh and Piglet and Christopher Robin played it in The House at Pooh Corner *by A. A. Milne.*

have Latin names, too. The house mouse, for example, is called *Mus musculus,* and man is called *Homo sapiens.*"

"Who made up all the names?" I asked.

"Different scientists," said Mr. Bloom. "I think that most of the names for flowers were made up by the Swedish botanist Carolus Linnaeus."

"He's the one whose flower I'm named after!"

"That's right," said Mr. Bloom. "When he was your age, he was already studying plants and animals. When he grew up, he wrote scientific books and arranged plants and animals according to family groups. That was more than two hundred years ago, but we are still using the Linnaean system today."

"Who are the *Tussilagos* related to?"

"Dandelions, for example. You can almost see that. They both belong to the great flower family the *Compositae.* They're made up of tiny flower clusters."

"Flower clusters!" I said. "But a coltsfoot is only one flower . . ."

"Look through the magnifying glass. Each coltsfoot is really hundreds of small flowers. The ones in the center are male flowers, and the ones surrounding them are females."

"What about the leaves?" I asked, running back to the water's edge to have a look. But there were no leaves, not a single one!

"The leaves come in the summer," said Mr. Bloom. "Then there will be buds, too, but they won't bloom until the following summer. This is last year's flower." – When we got home, I filled an egg cup with water. "This is for you, little *Farfara,*" I whispered.

The blackbird

Another sign of spring is the blackbird, who sings in our back yard early in the morning. (It's the male who has the beautiful voice.) The blackbirds that I hear in March are the ones that have spent the winter here. The ones that flew south won't be back until April. The blackbird was once a shy forest bird, but now he is a citydweller. He is an expert at finding worms in the grass. First he sits and *listens* for worms, and then he attacks! He also likes apples, especially if they're a little rotten. He prefers eating on the ground, so he doesn't usually visit my window feeder. The female is dark brown with a brown bill.

17

What are you allowed to pick?

And what are you *not* allowed to pick?

🍂*Wildflowers:* Hundreds of plants and wildflowers have died out, or are in danger of dying out, because people have picked so many of them. You can get a list of *threatened* and *endangered* plants from the library. *Never* pick any of these.

🍂The best way to save our wildflowers is to enjoy them where they are. If you want to take one home, why not do a drawing of it or take a picture with your camera?

🍂But if you still want to pick a wildflower (for your herbarium or to make a garland, for example), choose a common one, like an oxeye daisy or a dandelion. Cut it with scissors; don't pull up the roots.

🍂You may pick flowers only on your own property or your friends' property. (Ask first!) You are not allowed to remove or damage anything in public places such as national, state, or local parks and nature centers. You can learn more about this in a book called *Endangered Plants* by Dorothy Hogner, or by asking someone at your state park or nature center.

Vernal equinox

The vernal equinox is the twenty-four-hour period at the end of March when day and night are equally long. You can look it up on a calender. It usually comes around March 21.

After that, the days start getting longer and longer. And since the sun is out more, the days get warmer. Spring has come!

In the middle of the summer, around June 21, the days are at their longest. That's called the summer solstice. In northern countries, the sun never goes down at all. Tourists from all over the world go there to see the "midnight sun."

After that, the days start getting shorter again. Around September 23, there is an autumnal equinox, when night and day are equally long again.

And guess what happens around the twenty-first of December? That's right, night is at its longest. It's called the winter solstice. In countries very far north, the sun doesn't come up at all!

All of this is the result of the way the earth rotates around the sun. But that's too hard for me to explain. You'll have to get a globe and a grown-up to help you.

P.S. In the Southern Hemisphere, everything is just the opposite. Midsummer comes in December!

APRIL

Spring! Spring! I've been out looking for
Anemone nemorosa (wood anemone, in Latin). It
belongs to the anemone family. *Nemorosa* means that it
grows in groves. Wood anemones bloom early, before
the trees get their leaves and block the light. A relative,
Anemone hepatica (or *Hepatica nobilis,* as it is now
called), blooms even earlier.

19

My little  garden turns

Mr. Brush and I bought some seed packets at a nursery. It's still too early to plant any seeds outside, but we usually start our plants indoors and then move them outside later.

For a long time now, I've been thinking about making a little indoor garden. I bought some packets with garden cress, mustard, and grass seed, and one with peanuts.

Then I spread out some soil on a big metal lid that I'd found (a watertight tray or a big cake pan is good, too). I planted the seeds in little rows and squares. Around the edges I poked down some wheat kernels (leftover birdseed), split peas, and a couple of scarlet-runner beans. I planted the peanuts in a tiny flowerpot that I put in the middle. I made neat little paths of sand, and put in a little plastic gardener. Two tiny plastic rabbits moved in, too. The whole thing looked really neat and tidy.

But that didn't last long! After four days, the new sprouts had pushed their way through the soil, and all the neat little rows were a big mess. Everything was growing wild.

After a week, my little garden had turned into a jungle! The peas were climbing over the edge; the scarlet runners were winding themselves around the wheat and cress bushes. I could hardly see the gardener, and where were the rabbits?

After a couple of weeks, the whole thing was such a mess that I decided to get rid of it. I cut the wheat, mustard, and cress and used them in a salad. The peas and scarlet runners I planted in Mr. Brush's garden. Mine was a short-lived garden, but it was fun while it lasted. I still have the peanut plant on my windowsill.

Peanut

into a jungle

Street games

"Now you *have to* tell me what kind of games you and Mr. Bloom played when you were kids," I told Mr. Brush. "And don't say you don't remember."

Mr. Brush thought for a minute, and then he remembered something. He and Mr. Bloom used to play gutterball. You can play it only where there's a runoff gutter across the sidewalk from the drainpipe to the street. You need a tennis ball. Mr. Bloom had to come out to the sidewalk and help demonstrate.

You stand on opposite sides of the sidewalk gutter (two giant steps away from it) and throw the ball toward the gutter. If you throw it right, the ball will bounce back and you'll get a point. But usually the ball bounces over to the other player, and you lose your turn.

"The first one to get ten points wins," said Mr. Bloom.

"Are you sure about that?" said Mr. Brush. "I thought we used to go up to twenty."

NO POINT, TOO BAD ...   ONE POINT, HOORAY!

The magpie

A couple of magpies are building a big nest in my maple tree. It has a "roof" and a side entrance.

"*Scha-scha-scha,*" laugh the magpies, so the smaller birds are scared to death and fly away.

Magpies are supposed to be the only animals that wouldn't go into Noah's Ark. They sat up on the roof and laughed, instead. There are lots of stories about magpies. There is even an opera about them, called *The Thievish Magpie.* I've heard that they sometimes carry bits of glass, bottle tops, and other shiny things up to their nests, like little thieves.

It's hard to get near a magpie, because it just flies away. I usually watch my magpies through a pair of binoculars. Then I can see how their black feathers shine in rich shades of blue and green and purple. Young magpies have shorter tails than older ones.

The magpie is a common city bird. It's happy living around people. If it was less common, people would probably think the magpie was something really special.

MAY

Look what Mr. Bloom and I found up in the attic! Can you guess what it is? It's something that comes in handy this time of year, when lots of things are coming up. Out of the ground, I mean.

And lots of things have to be put down into the ground, too. Wow, have we ever got a lot to do!

"And just then they got a glimpse of the first butterfly. Now everybody knows that if the first butterfly you see is yellow, then it will be a happy summer. If it is white, then the summer will be calm. (We won't even mention black and brown butterflies – they are much too sad.)"
From The Magician's Hat *by Tove Jansson*

I press my first flower

It was Mr. Bloom's old flower press that we found in the attic. And a vasculum, a metal case for carrying plant samples.

We also brought down Mr. Bloom's herbarium. Carefully we untied the ribbons on the stiff folders. On each yellowed page was a pressed plant. There were hundreds of them.

"Did you press all of these yourself?"

"Yes," said Mr. Bloom. "In my day, children had to press plants during summer vacation to show them at school in the fall. Too bad they don't do that anymore; it was a good way to study nature. And what cheap entertainment!"

"I want to press a flower right away!" I said.

"Well then, this can be your very own plant press," said Mr. Bloom.

Which flower is it?

That's what Mr. Bloom asked when I came home with my first find in the vasculum.

"It's a forget-me-not," I said. "Anybody can see that. Look, they are the same blue color as the sky."

Mr. Bloom got out his flower identification book. It has descriptions of almost every flower. Oh no! There were *seven* different kinds of forget-me-nots in his book.

"We'll start by getting out the magnifying glass," said Mr. Bloom. "And then we'll use Linnaeus' gender system, because that's how this book is organized."

In Mr. Bloom's book I could see what the different parts of a flower were called. We started by counting the number of stamens. There were five. Turn to

OH, A LITTLE LOUSE GOT PRESSED BY MISTAKE!

page 11, it said. Tree, bush, or plant, it wanted to know.

"Plant, of course," I answered.

And the petals, are they touching? Are they blue with a yellow ring of small bumps? Are the hairs on the calyx straight and tight? In that case, according to the flower identification book, it could only be a *Myosotis palustris,* a genuine forget-me-not.

(I'm just pretending it was that easy. Without Mr. Bloom, I would never have figured out that it was a genuine forget-me-not.)

"*Palustris* means that it grows where it's humid," Mr. Bloom explained.

"That's right," I said. "I got my feet wet when I picked it."

I put the forget-me-not between two pieces of blotting paper and placed it in the press. (Old newspaper works, too.) Then I put on the cover and tied it down tightly with the cord.

At first I changed the papers every day, then once a week. After three weeks, the forget-me-not was dry, and it didn't feel cold any longer. (A thicker plant would have taken longer to dry.)

We mounted the forget-me-not on a piece of heavy paper with adhesive tape. (Ordinary Scotch tape is not good for plants.) Then I made a label with its name, family, growth, location, and the date. Now I have a herbarium, too.

I compared my forget-me-not with Mr. Bloom's. His paper had yellowed, but his flower didn't look any older than mine. Even though it was pressed over fifty years ago, Mr. Bloom's forget-me-not was still sky-blue!

MYOSÓTIS PALÚSTRIS
GENUINE FORGET-ME-NOT
Family: BORAGINACEAE
Location:
    JOHNSON FARM
Habitat: MARSHLAND
5/27 1988 Linnea

25

Get out the seeds and plants

It's time for planting in Mr. Brush's garden! We already had the seeds we needed, but now we had to stop off at a plant nursery. That's where plants are started from tiny seeds and nursed in greenhouses until they are big enough to be sold and planted in people's gardens.

Mr. Brush picked out the plants he wanted. Some of them looked really scrawny – nothing more than a clump of soil with a stick poking out. But Mr. Brush said that the ugliest ones could later turn out to be the nicest.

Next door to the nursery was a botanical garden, a sort of park with different kinds of plants in it. Each one had a Latin name tag. Some plants, from warm and humid countries, had to be kept in a special greenhouse.

"How is Victoria doing?" Mr. Brush asked.

"Growing like crazy," said Manny, who takes care of the plants in the greenhouses.

"Come over to the Victoria House and have a look."

"We don't have time today," said Mr. Brush. "We've got to get busy planting."

(Oh no! I would have loved to see who this Victoria was . . .)

"Well, come back in the summer," said Manny. "Then you'll see something special."

Dig, sow, plant, water

It took us all day to get everything planted. Mr. Brush worked mostly with the vegetables, and I took the flowers. I sowed hollyhock and marigold seeds, sweet peas and scarlet runners. The note on the seed packets tells you what to do. (And they were so pretty, I saved them!) I also transplanted the scarlet runners from my little homemade jungle.

A little over a week later, I could see a bit of green poking up where I'd planted the hollyhocks and scarlet runners, but the sweet peas were real slowpokes.

"It's a good thing they don't all come up at the same time," Mr. Brush said. "The summer is long."

We make nettle soup

Just think – stinging nettles don't sting after they've been made into soup. We put on gloves and picked two pints of small, delicate nettles, growing here and there in the garden. (The larger leaves aren't good.)

Then we rinsed them well, and put them in 2½ cups boiling water, along with a bouillon cube. After five minutes, we took out the nettle leaves.

Mr. Brush melted a tablespoon butter (it might have been a little more) in another saucepan. Then he stirred in one tablespoon flour and some of the nettle broth. When it was all mixed, he stirred in the rest of the broth.

The nettles had cooled by then, and I chopped them finely on a cutting board along with some chives. That went into Mr. Brush's pan, along with some salt and pepper.

We let the soup cook about five minutes more. Then we poured it into bowls, added sliced hard-boiled eggs, and we were ready to eat.

"My poor grandmother," I said, as we started eating. "She lives way up north where the nettles haven't come out yet."

"You can mail some to her," said Mr. Brush. "They'll get there before they have a chance to wilt."

So I picked some nettles for Grandma, and put them first in a plastic bag and then in an envelope. I sent the recipe along, too, just in case.

Recipe for 2
2 PINTS NETTLES
2½ CUPS WATER
1 BOUILLON CUBE
1-2 TABLESPOONS BUTTER
1 TABLESPOON FLOUR
CHIVES
SALT AND PEPPER

The chaffinch

It is the second most common bird where I live. (The willow warbler is the most common, but for some strange reason, I never see any.) The chaffinch is a migratory bird, but a few of the males stay through the winter. The chaffinch builds its nest in branch crotches. It makes a little bowl-like shape of moss, spiderwebs, and hair (some of it mine perhaps). The female's colors are a little paler than the male's but she has white-tipped wings, just like his. *"Fink, fink,"* says the male chaffinch to the female. That means "Come here." In Paris, they probably say, *"Oui, oui"* (that means "yes, yes" in French).

27

Kite weather!

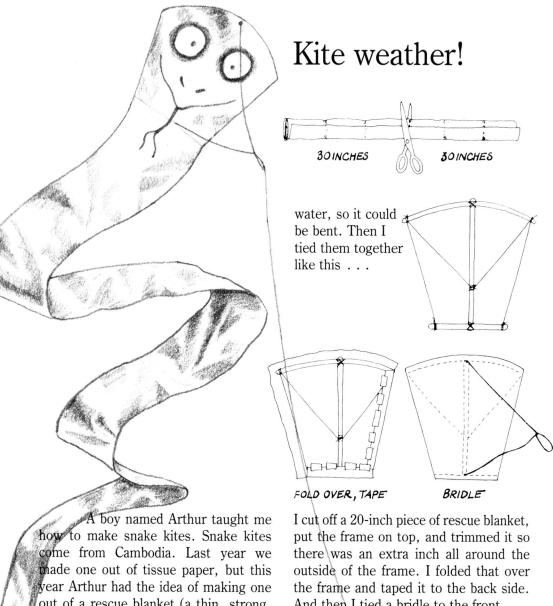

30 INCHES   30 INCHES

water, so it could
be bent. Then I
tied them together
like this . . .

FOLD OVER, TAPE   BRIDLE

A boy named Arthur taught me how to make snake kites. Snake kites come from Cambodia. Last year we made one out of tissue paper, but this year Arthur had the idea of making one out of a rescue blanket (a thin, strong, silver Mylar sheet that we bought at a sporting-goods store).

The trick was to cut it in two without having it wind up in more than one direction. Now we each had half a rescue blanket. I made a frame out of three lightweight sticks (10, 18, and 26 inches long). First I soaked the longest one in

I cut off a 20-inch piece of rescue blanket, put the frame on top, and trimmed it so there was an extra inch all around the outside of the frame. I folded that over the frame and taped it to the back side. And then I tied a bridle to the front.

10 INCHES   8   6   4   2

I cut the tail from the rest of the folded rescue blanket. I taped the pieces together, starting with the widest piece and working down. When I finished, it had a 25-foot tail. I glued on the weird eyes.

LOOK AT MY SILVER SNAKE!

JUNE

Guess what I have on my head. *Taraxacum vulgare!*
I made the garland myself (without a string, of course).
"Oh no, weeds!" is what most people say about dandelions.
Not me. They always make me think of Nickie (a rabbit I
once knew). He loved fresh dandelion leaves. People can eat
them, too (in salads, for example).
Look, here comes a bumblebee! What luck!!!

29

I make a garland

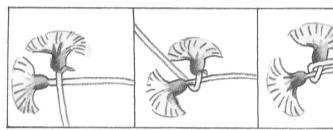

You're not always going to have a wire or string with you, so it's good to know how to make a garland without them.

You can use any flower (or grass) you want, as long as it has a flexible stem. If you use small or delicate flowers, take several at a time. If you choose dandelions, as I did, don't forget that you can get stains on your clothes from the sap in the stem.

The mute swan

Those fairy-tale birds really exist! This time of year, swans usually have newly hatched babies – a row of little gray downy balls that peep in the world's tiniest voices. But their parents hiss at me when I give their babies bread. Some swan parents teach their young to move into town for the winter, instead of flying south. There's food for them in the city. The babies grow fast, but they won't get white until next summer. The whopper swan has a yellow bill without a bump, but I've never seen one here in the city.

(without any string)

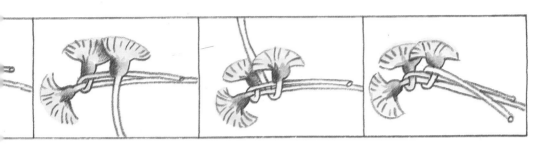

Just look at the pictures above. (It would sound harder than it is if I tried to explain it in words.)

Now try it on for size. The ends should overlap a little. Tie them with a strong blade of grass in a couple of places. And break off the stems that are too long.

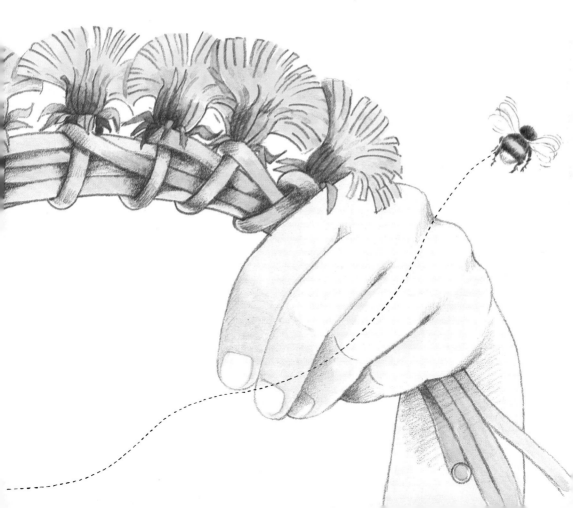

A red clover's best friend

Here comes a bumblebee. And here's a red clover (we'll pretend that my pressed clover is really growing in a meadow). The bumblebee is looking for sweet clover nectar. But will he be able to find it? A red clover has extra-deep hiding places for its nectar.

Well, that's okay, because a bumblebee has an extra long tongue. Almost no other insect can reach all the way down into a red clover.

When a bumblebee sits on a clover, some pollen sticks to its body. When it moves on to the next clover, some pollen falls off and fertilizes the flower. And as everyone knows, without fertilization there won't be any seeds or any new clover next year. So it's lucky that we have bumblebees.

Mr. Bloom told me all about that. And he told me about the first bees in the spring, the extra-large ones. They are queens, who wake up from their winter nap and fly out looking for places to lay their eggs (which were fertilized when they mated last fall). They especially like abandoned field-mice nests near drainage ditches.

But nowadays drainage ditches are usually covered, so there aren't as many for the bees. And where fields are sprayed with insecticide, there aren't many bumblebees, either. So what will happen to all the red clover?

Well, let's say the queen bee somehow manages to find a good place to lay her eggs. She will have her hands full before her children become fully-grown worker bees. They are all females, smaller than she is. Some will turn into queens. Later in the summer the males

are born. They come out only once, to mate with the new queens. Then they die. The workers and the old queen die, too. Only the young fertilized queen bees survive the winter. That's how a year looks in the life of a bumblebee.

THE BUMBLEBEE CARRIES HOME POLLEN ON ITS BACK LEGS

Summer solstice

According to the Almanac, the summer solstice is on June 21. On that day, the sun is out longer than any other day of the year.

Mr. Brush and Mr. Bloom and I celebrated the summer solstice with a party in the garden. I had made garlands for all three of us.

Buttercups last all year

Here is my pressed buttercup. It's related to the wood anemone. Grazing animals think that buttercups taste bad, so they leave them alone. I usually pick big bouquets of buttercups, tie them together with a string, and hang them upside down to dry. It's best to hang them in the dark.

The dried flowers are still a pretty yellow color. Imagine having buttercups in the middle of winter!

"Do you like butter?" asks Mr. Brush, holding a buttercup under my chin. "I see you do, because your chin turned yellow." (I do love butter, but your chin turns yellow even if you don't.)

33

Rhubarb, rhubarb

In Mr. Brush's garden, things are growing so fast right now that you can almost hear them. The apple trees and lilacs are in bloom. And something is ripe already: rhubarb. Rhubarb has the biggest leaves I've ever seen*, but you can only eat the stem. The leaves are actually *poisonous*. Rhubarb isn't just delicious (as compote with ice cream, for example); it's good for:

   hats

(especially when it's raining),

   plates

(especially for strawberries),

   conversation

(especially if you want to sound like a crowd, and you're really only three people. Just try saying "Rhubarb, rhubarb, rhubarb"), and

   in a vase

(especially when it's sunny; the light that filters through the leaves can make a whole room green).

* That used to be the biggest leaf I'd ever seen!

My rhubarb compote

Preheat the oven to 375°F.

   Wash 3 pieces of rhubarb and strip off the outside skin (their "silk dresses").

   Grease an ovenproof baking dish with butter. Cut the rhubarb into 2-inch pieces and put them in the dish. Sprinkle 1/4 cup sugar across the top, and bake the rhubarb in the middle of the oven 20 to 30 minutes.

   Serve the compote when it has cooled off a little, but not completely. The recipe makes enough for two if you add some vanilla ice cream. Yum! Yum!

The best place to go, when you want to get out of the city, is the beach. What can you do there? Hunt for treasures, of course, especially after a storm, when lots of stuff has floated up on land.

I like to make reed boats, too, like the one you see here. Just stick the point of a reed leaf into the stem and it's ready to sail.

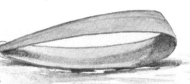

35

My beach treasures

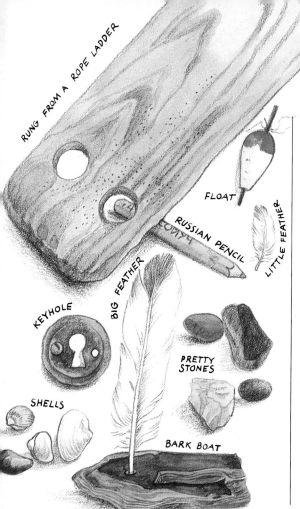

RUNG FROM A ROPE LADDER

FLOAT

RUSSIAN PENCIL

LITTLE FEATHER

BIG FEATHER

KEYHOLE

PRETTY STONES

SHELLS

BARK BOAT

"What should we do now?" said Tommy.

"I don't know what you are going to do," said Pippi, "but I'm not going to just lie around. I happen to be a treasure hunter, and a treasure hunter never has a dull moment."

From Pippi Longstocking *by Astrid Lindgren*

I agree with Pippi Longstocking. And the best place for treasure hunting is a beach. The place is crawling with treasures – but they aren't treasures until somebody finds them! Today I found:

A little float (I hadn't gone more than a few feet; probably a really strong fish had broken off the fishing line) and a piece of wood, floating near the shore. Not just an ordinary piece, though. It was silver-gray and smoothed by the waves. On each end there were two big holes (plus about a thousand tiny worm-holes). It must have been a rung from a boat ladder. A useful treasure – once I decide what to do with it!

Oh! I almost missed a treasure: a tur-

The black-headed gull

"Crey, crey, creck-creck-creck-creck-creck," screech the black-headed gulls, wherever they go. They are the most common gulls, easy to recognize by their chocolate-brown heads, which look black from a distance. In the winter, the brown turns white, except for a dark spot behind the ear. Some black-headed gulls fly south as early as July, but many stay in the city, where there's food, all winter.

quoise pencil, with Russian writing on it! Just think, maybe a Russian sailor, way out at sea . . . No, wait, it was probably a little Russian girl, who got to go along on the boat. There she is, sitting on deck with all her colored pencils and some drawing paper. Oh no! The boat tips, and the colored pencils roll toward the railing! She manages to save them all, except for the turquoise.

I found some other things, too: unusual stones, shells, seaweed, and a keyhole. I found a piece of bark with a hole in it, and some feathers. The biggest one fit exactly into the hole, and it became a bark sailboat.

After that, I found a piece of china with a blue pattern. When I picked it up, I spotted four more pieces. And then even more! All of them had different patterns. They looked old. *How in the world* did they ever get here? China dishes can't float. Maybe some people were having a picnic, and they started fighting and smashed all the dishes. Or was there someone working in the kitchen who broke them and didn't dare tell anyone but just threw the pieces into the water?

By now I had collected so many pieces that I had to put them in my hat. I know what I'll do with them! Wait and see . . .

What's that shining in the reeds?

How stupid to throw away an old bottle, I thought. But then I saw that it was no ordinary bottle, but a bottle with a message in it! It was from two girls who wrote that their names were Vera and Windflower and they were exactly my age.

"Dear Finder of Our Secret Message, Please send us a letter right away (by regular mail), and tell us where you found this Secret Message. Hope you are nice, because here comes the secret part."

(I can't tell you what they said next, since it is a secret.)

I wrote right back to Vera and Windflower (by regular mail), but I also put their message back in the bottle along with one of my own. The next time we were out far from shore in our boat, I threw the bottle overboard. I wonder what will happen.

Elder-blossom nectar

TRUE ELDER   POISONOUS ELDER

I know where there's an elder tree. A long time ago, people used elder for medicine and to scare away ghosts and witches. I use elder blossoms to make nectar.

Elder trees can grow wild or in gardens. One kind is *poisonous*. Its flowers are greenish-yellow and grow in *pointed* (grape-like) clusters that have no smell; you *don't* want to use those!

True elder has pale yellow flowers in flat *rounded* clusters that give off a strong smell. They make delicious nectar.

Here's what I did:

I picked 25 large flower clusters and put them in a big jar.

Then I sliced 1½ lemons and put them in a pot with 2 pints water and 2 pounds sugar. I heated the mixture until it boiled, and then I poured it over the elder blossoms. I covered the jar and let it stand for 3 days.

Now it was time to strain the nectar and pour it into bottles. I strained it through a coffee filter into a pitcher. Then I corked the bottles.

IMPORTANT: The bottles must be *well washed* and filled all the way to the top. Otherwise, the nectar will get moldy. If you do it right, your nectar will last for six months in the refrigerator. An opened bottle has to be used up within a month, but that shouldn't be a problem!

P.S.
There are lots of other things you can do with elder: make elder-blossom sandwiches (not bad – really!), fry flower clusters dipped in batter (not so great), or just look at the pretty little flowerets with a magnifying glass, or read Hans Christian Andersen's story "The Elder-tree Mother."

Recipe
25 ELDER BLOSSOM CLUSTERS
1½ LEMONS
2 LBS. SUGAR
1 QUART WATER

It's time to harvest the vegetables in Mr. Brush's garden. I like the snow peas best! Eat them by pulling them through your teeth. That way you get both the peas and the good part from the inside of the pod. You can cook them a little first if you like. I did each pod in an egg cup filled with melted butter. What a treat in the August moonlight!

We also went back to the Victoria House. Now it was time . . .

Victorias's secret life

The flowers are in bloom now, too

Here are my hollyhocks and marigolds. The sweet peas are also in bloom. My scarlet runners have already bloomed, and they are starting to get giant pods.

The common swift

A swift looks like a large swallow. It isn't related to the swallow. It's a city bird, yet I never see it, because it lives high up under the roof tiles or in church towers. It spends most of its time flying; it can even sleep while flying. Sometimes, when the parents are gone a long time searching for food (insects), their babies faint. But it doesn't matter; they can survive that way for several weeks until their parents come back. At this time of the year, the young are grown and ready to fly to Africa.

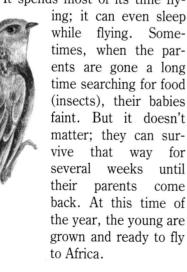

It wasn't all that strange that Thumbelina could ride on a water lily. After all, in the fairy tale she was only one inch tall. But now I have seen a water lily pad that could carry a *real* child. I went back to the "plant museum" (the botanical garden) and visited Manny, who takes care of Victoria in the round Victoria greenhouse.

Victoria is a giant water lily. She is named *Victoria cruziana* after an English queen and a South American general.

Just now, the pads are at their biggest. They look almost artificial: *enormous* pads with rolled-up edges. They can be up to six feet across. Manny knows that they can carry real children; he's tried it.

Victoria blooms only once, at night, with a white flower. The next night the flower turns pink. After that, it wilts and sinks to the bottom of the pond.

Manny told me about Victoria's wild and secret life on the Amazon River in South America. There, the seed cases eventually break open on the river bottom, and the seeds float up to the surface. Then they float away on the river current, so they won't crowd the mother plant.

Once settled, the seeds sink down to the bottom again and start to grow. By then it's the dry season, with just enough water in the river for the new plants to be able to reach up to the surface.

Next comes the rainy season. As the river rises, Victoria's stem grows as much as it can. That way, it will always reach up to the surface of the water; otherwise, it would drown.

Here in the greenhouse pond, Manny has to help Victoria. In the fall he collects the seed cases on the bottom of the pond and saves them through the winter.

On March 12 (Victoria's name day), he plants the seeds in small flowerpots underwater. The water temperature has to be exactly 85° F. or the seeds won't grow.

By early May, the plants are big enough to be moved over to the big pond, first in shallow and then in deeper and deeper water.

In July and early August, Victoria blooms, secretly, since the greenhouse is closed at night. But we saw the buds!

"Tonight's the night," said Manny.

Victoria's flower is the bud in the center. The blue flowers are another kind of water lily.

41

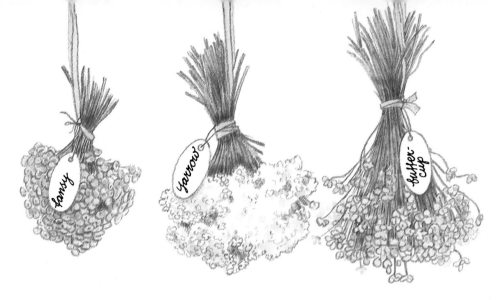

Long live summer!

Summer is soon over, if you don't save some of it for winter. You can do that by drying cut flowers. Some turn out nice; others will simply fall apart and lose all their color. The *buttercup* dries well (see page 33) and so does the *common tansy*. It looks like a daisy without any petals.

Then there's *yarrow*. If you pick them when they're blooming, the bouquet will be white; if you pick them later, it will be brown.

To dry a flower, I remove the leaves first. Then I press the flowers together, cut the stems the same length, and tie them tightly with a ribbon. The bouquet looks like a little ball.

Hang it upside down to dry (a dark place is best). Sometimes I make a garland of flowers (see page 30) and dry that. A garland I made out of grass turned out really nice, too.

In fact, I dry just about everything: maple seed pods, chestnut shells, acorns. And I'm pretty satisfied with a necklace I made out of rowanberries.

SEPTEMBER

Hurray for all the city trees! I've been collecting their leaves and pressing them. In September, night and day become equally long again. And the darker the nights, the better you can see the stars.

Autumn equinox

43

The life of a city tree

My maple tree's trunk is so thick that Mr. Bloom and I can barely reach around it *together*. Mr. Bloom says it might be as much as two hundred years old. Just think, it might have been planted when George Washington was President!

It's fun to think about the future, too. A little baby tree planted today will make a big beautiful tree for my children and grandchildren!

"Strictly speaking, a newly planted tree is no baby," says Mr. Bloom. "It's more like a teenager. By the time a tree is planted in the city, it has usually spent about thirteen years in a nursery, where lots of people have taken care of it. It's been watered and fertilized and had its top and roots trimmed every year. Otherwise, it would have become tall and scrawny.

A tree has to be thick and strong to survive the tough life in the city: with paving, engine exhaust, and dirt aboveground, and pipes, cables, parking garages, and cement underground. But a tree has plenty of soil under all the asphalt, even if you can't see it.

Trees that line sidewalks and streets don't live as long as park trees. They die after fifty to eighty years. My maple is lucky. It lives in a little grassy yard between two buildings. It hardly grows at all anymore. Maple trees grow a lot the first forty years, and then they slow down.

Without trees, the city would be really depressing. Trees are good for lots of things:

housing (for birds, squirrels, etc.)
climbing
resting under
cleaning the air
absorbing noise
showing off the seasons
helping us to find our way through all those buildings
looking at.

We have to take care of our trees, even the small ones. If we don't, there won't be any trees for our children and grandchildren. Or our great-grandchildren!"

The crow

Caw, caw, caw! I just heard the first autumn croaking of the crows. I know all-black crows exist, but I've never seen any. It's difficult to tell crows from ravens (they're larger) and rooks (they're smaller). Magpies are also crows, but they don't look like anything but magpies. Crows build their nests in city trees out of twigs, soil, and moss. The female lays up to five blue-green spotted eggs. After they hatch, both parents work at feeding the young. By this time of year, they are grown and out of the nest.

44

A little atlas of leaves

I pressed the leaves from thirteen city trees:

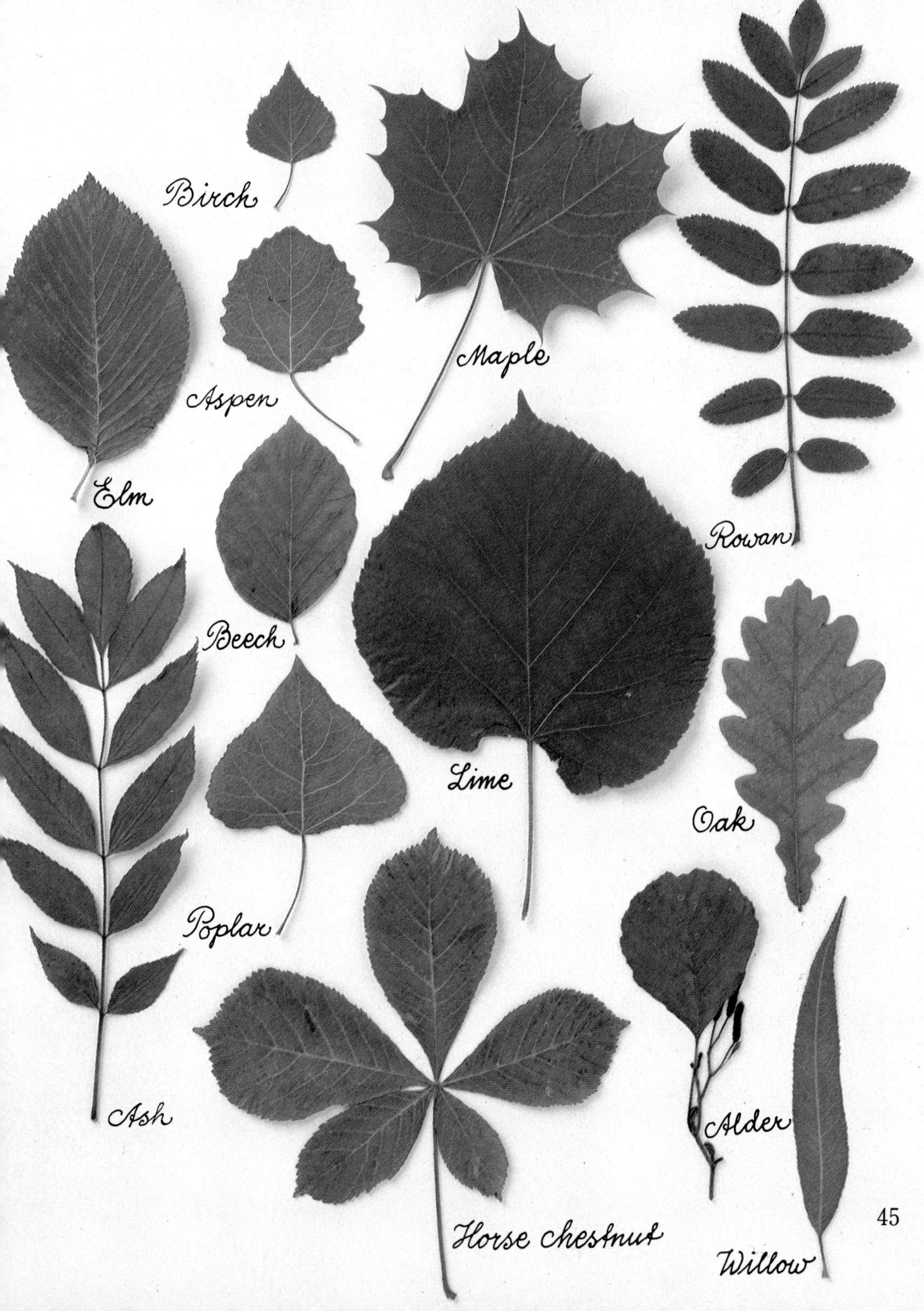

Birch

Aspen

Maple

Rowan

Elm

Beech

Lime

Oak

Poplar

Ash

Horse chestnut

Alder

Willow

Look at the stars!

Wow! So many stars! I saw more and more of them as my eyes got used to the dark. I read somewhere that you can see two thousand stars with the naked eye, but with a telescope you can see millions. Dark, clear nights like the ones we have now are the best time to see them.

I spotted the Big Dipper right away. It's part of Ursa Major. That means "Greater Bear" in Latin, but it looks more like a giraffe.

If I draw a line through the two stars on the end of the Big Dipper and continue it straight up, I come to the bright North Star (Polaris). It's almost directly above the North Pole, and it's part of the constellation called the Little Dipper (Ursa Minor, the "Lesser Bear").

What is a star? Generally, it's a gas cloud, so hot that it glows. The sun is our closest star. The earth is not a star; it's a planet that rotates around the sun. Planets don't shine; they only reflect the sun's light. Other planets in our solar system are Mars and Venus. The stars that I can see are suns in other solar systems.

The bright path of stardust in the sky is called the Milky Way. It's made up of billions of stars so far away that I can't begin to imagine it. Not only that. Beyond the Milky Way that we see are other galaxies that we can't see! Oh well, the universe is so incredibly gigantic that . . . I think I'll go home and go to bed.

OCTOBER

My favorite tree in the whole city is probably my maple tree. Right now its leaves are starting to turn yellow and red. Soon they'll all fall off, and I'll be right there to pick up the prettiest ones. I'll use them to make a beautiful autumn crown. I'll show you how. And I'll also tell you about a bird that isn't listed in my bird book, and about some other interesting animals that live here in the city. Some people scream when they see them . . .

My autumn crown

1. First I cut off all the thick stem ends. Then I folded the *first* leaf down the middle.

2. I poked a hole through both halves and pushed the stem of the *second* leaf through the hole.

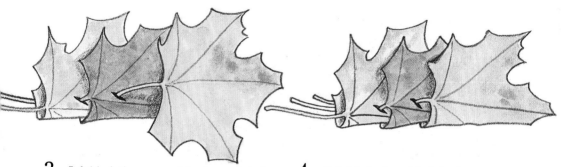

3. I folded the second leaf around the first one and stuck the stem of the *third* leaf through the other two.

4. I folded the third leaf around the other two. I did the same thing with all the other leaves. That was easy, wasn't it?

LOCK IT WITH A STEM

5. When I had woven 22 leaves together, I tried on the crown. It fit perfectly, so I overlapped the ends and stuck a stem through to "lock" them together. It looks nice, doesn't it? I think I'll make one for Mr. Bloom's birthday, because there won't be any flowers to pick for him then.

Why do leaves turn yellow?

"Your maple doesn't need its leaves in the winter," said Mr. Bloom. "They would actually do more harm than good. That's true for most broad leaf trees (deciduous trees). It would be too hard to keep all those leaves alive when winter comes; it's more important that the roots, trunk, and branches survive."

The tiny particles in the leaves that make them green are called *chlorophyll*. With the help of the sun's energy, chlorophyll makes some of my maple's "food." But chlorophyll only works when it's light and warm, so a maple tree has to pack a "bag lunch" for winter. The trunk and branches suck up all the chlorophyll, nourishment, and sap from the leaves.

What about the yellow color in the leaves? Well, it was actually there all the time, but we couldn't see it because of the green. There was even some red in the leaves that we couldn't see until now.

After the maple tree has taken what it needs from the leaves, their stems loosen from the branches. And then one fine day, the first autumn leaf flutters to the ground. Nothing is left but a scar.

But inside the branch, just at the place where the stem used to be, a tiny little leaf is already waiting for spring. I think that's nice to know.

The pigeon

Thousands of years ago people tamed wild rock doves. Our own city pigeons are the wild descendants of those tamed rock doves. There are no big rocks for them to fly up to, but the city rooftops have become the pigeons' rocks. They build their nests in drainpipes and in other cozy places. Pigeons don't like modern buildings without nooks and crannies.

Pigeons can have babies from February to November, several broods a year. The male and female take turns sitting on the eggs and feeding the newly hatched babies with "pigeon milk," a white liquid that they cough up from their stomachs.

That's about all I know about pigeons, since they aren't listed in my bird book. I don't think that's fair to the nice pigeon who prances around on my windowsill!

This is how city animals live

A *Sciurus vulgaris* lives right in my maple tree. He (or she) is a squirrel and a world-champion nutcracker. Right now his fur is turning gray, because he is getting his winter coat. In the spring, he'll be red again. He has one bad habit; he eats birds' eggs. Many other city animals are night creatures; it's nice that you can see the squirrel during the day.

For example, I never see a *Mus musculus,* or house mouse (see page 17), even though I'm sure there's one living in my house.

But late at night, when it's dark, you can run into a lot of *Pipistrellus pipistrellus* flapping around in the park. They aren't ghosts or birds, but bats. Soon they will be hanging upside down in some dark corner and starting to hibernate.

Don't even be surprised if you meet a *Vulpes vulpes* or a *Meles meles* in the park! I mean a fox or a badger, of course. They have actually started moving into the city. There are lots of good garbage cans here, and rats and mice to eat. And they think the parks are good places to dig burrows.

But now I want to tell you about the time I met a *Rattus norvegicus.* That's the most common city animal: the brown rat.

The rat and I were walking on the same sidewalk (he was on the inside). When I stopped at the crosswalk for a red light, the rat stopped, too. When the light turned green, we both crossed the street. But then the rat went into the park, and I went home.

Lots of people scream when they see a rat, but I think it's kind of exciting. It's too bad that they do so much damage. They dig tunnels, chew holes, and eat things up. And they spread disease. So *never* touch a rat. Remember, they live down in the sewers.

Brown rats reproduce quickly. A scientist studying rats once put a male and female rat in the same pen along with some food. After one year there were 862 rats in the pen! One female rat can have ten babies seven times a year; they can start having babies when they are only two and a half months old!

To begin with, brown rats were found only in Central Asia. They spread out, and now they can be found *everywhere* people live. Sometimes they traveled from place to place aboard ships, wiping out the local rat population when they arrived.

Have you ever read about the war between the black rats and the brown rats in a book by Selma Lagerlöf called The Wonderful Adventures of Nils?

NOVEMBER

Crisp autumn winds! Oh, how they blow! There went the last of the autumn leaves . . . But it's a nice time anyway, because now I'll take care of some things at home. First, Mr. Brush and I locked up his little garden house for the winter. Guess what I found when I got home? There was a postcard waiting for me with a picture of Carolus Linnaeus on it (he's the one who made up the Latin names for plants and animals). Two boys named Pelle and Olle had sent it. They had found my message in the bottle. Now we're going to be pen pals, all five of us: Vera, Windflower, Pelle, Olle, and me.

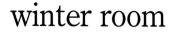

I fix up my winter room

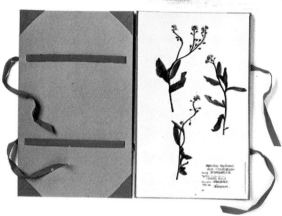

My room was a real mess. Pressed flowers, beach treasures, postcards, seed packets, dried acorns, and other stuff were lying all over the place. It's fun to collect things, but not when there's no place to put them. I'd better get this room in order!

My herbarium

I began with that. I took two thick pieces of cardboard and covered the corners with some red plastic tape. Next I punched holes in the cardboard and laced a ribbon through the holes. I put a label on the front, and then I was ready to put the pages with pressed plants inside the herbarium covers and tie the ribbons.

My matchbox chest of drawers

I needed four large and eight small (four in front, four in back) empty matchboxes. First I tied a wooden bead on each of the drawers with some strong thread. Then I glued all the boxes together, and covered the little chest of drawers with two layers of pretty wrapping paper that I had saved.

My bulletin board

I cut down a big piece of cardboard to fit into a frame that I had. Then I pasted a sheet of white drawing paper over the cardboard (I thought it looked nicer like that), and taped the cardboard all the way around the back of the frame. Now I had a bulletin board that was easy to stick pins into.

The first thing I hung up was the postcard of Linnaeus from Pelle and Olle, plus another one with Cartier-Bresson's "Picnic by the River Marne." I added a picture of the water-lily pond by Claude Monet (my idol, who's so good at painting flowers). There was still room for a couple of seed packets, some extra-special bookmarks, a few photos, and some of my beach treasures. You can see for yourself. When I get tired of those things, I can change the exhibit.

It really didn't take much for my room to be a nice place to be in again.

Bulb time!

Attention! Attention! It's time to plant bulbs if you want to have flowers blooming at Christmas! I've tried different kinds: *French daffodils, hyacinths, lilies of the valley, tulips.* But my favorite is *amaryllis.* Last year I got one that's called "Candy Floss," though it was the most expensive kind.

I planted it and watered it, exactly as it said in the directions. Candy Floss started growing right away, leaves first, bigger and bigger. I measured her every morning with a ruler; she grew about half an inch a day!

Then the stem started growing. And then, *another* stem! After five weeks it happened: Candy Floss bloomed! Four giant-size pink flowers on the first stem, just in time for Christmas. And on New Year's Day the other stem had four giant pink flowers. I've decided to choose an amaryllis this year, too.

The wild duck

The male mallard is beautifully "dressed," but the female is only a speckled brown color (except for a little blue on her wings). That way, she can hardly be seen when she's sitting on her eggs in the nest. The nest is usually built on a tuft of grass by the water or under a bush. But sometimes the female mallard lays her eggs in a hollow tree or an old crow's nest way up on land. Her babies have a real problem getting down to the water to learn to swim! First they have to *jump* down to the ground, because they haven't learned to fly yet. Usually everything turns out all right, since they are as light as little balls of down. And the police help them cross the street on the way down to the water. The babies begin to swim right away.

DECEMBER

My Christmas presents for Mr. Bloom and Mr. Brush are all ready, and now I'm wrapping them and making up poems to write on the packages. Then I'm going to make some decorations for the tree. What do you think of my surprise walnut? You open a walnut, take out the meat, put something else in it, glue it shut, and put it back in the bowl with the other nuts! I wonder who will get my Christmas elf walnut this year?

Christmas presents for my friends

Mr. Bloom is getting a plaster of Paris collage of beach treasures (see page 37). I started by screwing two hooks into a small cigar box. Then I mixed some plaster. *First* I poured some cold water in a plastic container, and then (the order is important) I slowly poured in the plaster until I could see small islands of it sticking out of the water. I counted to 20 before stirring it carefully with a plastic spoon, just a little bit. I poured the mixture into the cigar box and counted to 20 again. Then I quickly stuck the pieces of broken china (and some bits of broken mirror) into the plaster before it got too hard. It took a week for the picture to dry. I tied a string through the hooks, so that I could hang it up.

Important: Don't dump any plaster out into the sink or you will clog the drain!

I made Mr. Brush a picture out of an old sardine can that I had washed well and painted with enamel paint. Inside, I put a picture of myself dressed like a flower (taken on Mr. Brush's birthday last spring). Under the picture I made a little flower garden by sticking some dried tansies and yarrow into a little bit of clay.

December 21 or 22 is winter solstice, the longest night in the whole year. Above the polar circle the sun doesn't come up at all that day. In Vardö, a town in the north of Norway, they don't see the sun for two whole months. They shoot off a cannon the first time the sun comes back in January, and all the children get a sun holiday from school.

The bullfinch

There are many bullfinches in the city at this time of year. They usually live in the woods, but it's hard to find food there in the winter. The city has bird feeders – not to mention my maple tree! Bullfinches love the seeds inside maple pods. They think ash and rowan seeds are good, too. And when they've eaten those, they start nibbling on the trees' new spring buds. According to one old story, a bullfinch tried to help Jesus by pulling the thorns from his crown of thorns. Some drops of blood fell on the bird and colored his breast for all time. I think less must have fallen on his wife, because she is only a pale red. The same story is told about the robin redbreast.

57

Let's make Swedish heart baskets

CUT INTO STRIPS

FOLDED EDGE

Let's see. You start by folding two sheets of glossy paper (construction paper works, too), one red and one white. Then you cut out two half-heart shapes, like the one in the drawing. They'll be easier to weave if you make them larger than the sample pattern.

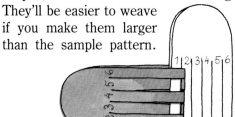

Then, holding one color in each hand, weave white strip number 1 *through* red strip number 6, around red 5, through red 4, around red 3, and so on. It's a little trickier to do the next white strip,

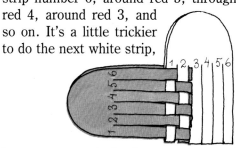

but you can push the first one up out of the way to give yourself more room. Weave white strip number 2 the same way, but start by going around red 6, *through* red 5, and so on. Continue weaving until you've used all the strips. Try it. It's a lot easier than it sounds. Next, cut out a strip of paper for a handle and glue or tape it on the inside of your heart basket. Now you can fill it with nuts and hang it on the tree.

Where do nuts come from?

Hazelnut   *Walnut*   *Soft-shell almond*   *Brazil nut*

Hazelnuts grow on hazel trees and bushes in most of Europe and the United States. "Yum!" say the squirrels and the birds.	*Walnut trees can be forty-five to sixty feet tall. The nut is inside a green fruit.*	*Almonds grow on small trees in Mediterranean countries, Asia, and California. Soft-shelled almonds are easy to crack, but sweet and bitter almonds have hard shells.*	*Brazil nuts grow on tall, tall trees in Brazil's forests. The fruit that holds the nut is as large as a head. The shell is hard as rock and difficult to crack.*

When you plant a nut, you never know if anything will come up or not. Hazelnuts, for example, have to be kept in a pot of sand in the refrigerator for three months before they can be planted. That way, they will think that winter has come and gone. Otherwise, they'll refuse to grow, which is actually very smart of them.

All nuts have to be rubbed with sandpaper before planting to make their shells thinner, so the sprout can break out of the shell.

Hazelnuts and walnuts don't like being indoors, so they should eventually be replanted outdoors. Brazil nuts and almonds can grow inside.

City Birds

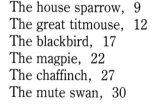

Thank you

Björn Berglund, who checked our facts,
and *Karl Johan Öholm* (Mr. Brush)
We also thank
Folke Björkbäck, Royal Museum of Natural History, Stockholm
Lennart Bolund, who showed us the titmouse bell
Mogens Lund, rat researcher, Copenhagen
Friedrich Drossel, City Parks, Haga Park, Stockholm
Laila Hellwig, who taught us to make maple-leaf crowns
Stig Sandell, Weibulls Nursery, Stockholm
Aage Sandqvist, Stockholm Observatory
Manfred Schrödl, Botanical Garden, Stockholm
Roland Staav, who told us about city birds

Rabén & Sjögren Stockholm

Illustrations copyright © 1982 by Lena Anderson
Originally published in Sweden by Rabén & Sjögren under the title
Linneas årsbok, text copyright © by Christina Björk
Library of Congress card number: 89-83540
First American edition 1989
Sixth printing 1995
Printed in Italy

ISBN 91 29 59176 7